December 1996

Dear Rinna,

Joy at this most
beautiful time of the
year.

Love
Tito Ben

Y0-BDI-267

A *Child's Treasury of*

PHILIPPINE
CHRISTMAS STORIES

a child's treasury of

PHILIPPINE

CHRISTMAS
STORIES

LIN ACACIO-FLORES
and
ANNETTE FLORES GARCIA

illustrated by
ALBERT GAMOS

Tahanan Books for Young Readers
MANILA

Published by Tahanan Books for Young Readers
A division of Tahanan Pacific, Inc.
P.O. Box 9079, MCS Mailing Center
1299 Makati City
Philippines

Text copyright © 1996 by Lin Acacio-Flores and Annette Flores Garcia
Illustrations copyright © 1996 by Albert Gamos
Designed by Therese K. Ng
Adobe Photoshop® by Reinard P. Santos

All rights reserved.
This book may not be reproduced, in whole or in part, in any form,
without written permission from the publisher. Address inquiries to
Tahanan Pacific, Inc., P.O.Box 9079, MCS Mailing Center,
1299 Makati City, Philippines

"The Bamboo Who Wanted to Be a Christmas Tree" won third prize in
the Don Carlos Palanca Memorial Awards for Literature category Short
Stories for Children (English) in 1993. This story and "Binny and the
Coconut Man" first appeared in the *Sunday Inquirer Magazine.*

National Library of the Philippines
Cataloging-in-Publication Data

Recommended entry:
Flores, Lin A.
   A child's treasury of Philippine
Christmas stories / by Lin Acacio-Flores and Annette Flores
Garcia.; illustrated by Albert Gamos. -
Makati City : Tahanan Books for
Young Readers, c1996. - 1 v

   1. Christmas stories - Philippines.
2. Children's stories, Philippine
(English). I. Garcia, Annette F.
II. Gamos, Albert. III. Title.

PL5546 1996 899.21'03 P962000001
ISBN 971-630-059-X

Printed in the Philippines by Island Graphics
I 3 5 4 2

Acknowledgments

Our grateful thanks to:
Monina Mercado and Lorna Kalaw-Tirol, for
showing us the way. And to Usman Imam Sheik-alaman,
Fe Attik E. Adil, and Mrs. Tamano for fact-checking
"The Sultan with a Heart of Stone;" and Juanita Trofeo
for doing the same for "The Christmas Ghosts of Vigan."

L.A.F. and A.F.G.

INTRODUCTION

Christmas in the Philippines is like a tall glass of *halo-halo*—made with Filipino sweetened beans, *pinipig, kaong, sabá, nangka*, Chinese *gulaman*, Spanish *leche flan*, and American ice cream—it's colorful to look at and delicious to eat!

Filipinos have adopted both the American Santa Claus and the Spanish Three Kings, who bring gifts to good children. Added to that are our *ninongs* and *ninangs*, who give us presents whether we have been good or bad.

We have the *panunuluyan*, an adaptation of the Mexican posadas or Christmas street drama.

Our *belen* is patterned after the French creche, only we dress the figures as though the Nativity had taken place within our shores.

We have the *pastores* of Legaspi City, who dress as shepherds and go from house to house, dancing and singing Spanish and Bicolano carols. In Cebu, carolers paint their faces to look like clowns or warriors. They perform acrobatic stunts, as well as dance and sing. In Negros and Panay, there are the *daigons* who incorporate skits and funny debates into their songs.

Our Christmas season is very long. We start decorating even before the beginning of Advent; we celebrate *misa de gallo* nine days before Christmas; we remember the Feast of the Holy Innocents on December 28; and after the New Year comes the Feast of the Three Kings and the Feast of the Christ Child. In the province of Nueva Ecija, December 25th is called *Pasko ng mga Bata*; January 1st is *Pasko ng mga Binata't Dalaga*; the Feast of the Three Kings is *Pasko ng mga Matatanda*.

Some Filipinos also consider the Chinese New Year part of the Christmas season. And we celebrate the moveable feast of the *Eid'l Fitr*, the Muslim counterpart of the Christian Christmas.

In short, Christmas in the Philippines is for everyone.

Within these pages, you will find stories of Christmas rituals and traditions from different parts of the Philippines. In keeping with the spirit of the book, we retained a number of Filipino words in these tales—words that, we feel, would have lost all their nuances in translation. A glossary is provided for quick and easy reference.

These stories are not folktales. They are works of fiction inspired by the happy, colorful bits and pieces that make up a Filipino Christmas.

Contents

A *Child's Treasury of*

PHILIPPINE

CHRISTMAS STORIES

THE BAMBOO WHO WANTED TO BE A CHRISTMAS TREE

ONCE upon a time, a bamboo tree lived with her three children by a winding stream. One misty December morning, Bamba, the youngest bamboo, awoke to a whining, piercing sound. Men were sawing branches off the pine trees nearby.

"They're going to make Christmas trees," Mama Bamboo said, welcoming the frightened birds into her waving arms.

"What are Christmas trees?" asked Bamba, nudging her older brothers, Boo and Ba, with her twiggy elbows.

"Christmas trees are pine trees that people take into their homes and make beautiful with lights and colored ornaments," replied Ba.

"You can see them at night if you stand tall and look over the ridge and at the town down below. But, of course, you're not tall enough," declared Boo loftily.

"I want to be a Christmas tree," Bamba announced.

Boo and Ba laughed. Even Mama Bamboo joined in, shaking her branches so hard the birds fled and Bamba cried.

Mama Bamboo calmed herself. "Look into the water, child. Do you look like a pine tree?"

Bamba peered tearfully at herself in the water and saw what she had always seen—a slender trunk, delicate branches, and narrow leaves in all shades of green, yellow, and brown. Pretty, yes, but nothing like a Christmas pine.

Mama Bamboo said comfortingly, "Someday, Bamba, you'll know what you're suited for. Boo has such strong limbs that he can carry a whole house on his shoulders. Ba has tough nodes. He will make a good footbridge, just like your father."

"Bamba will make good barbecue sticks," Boo snickered.

"Her fingers will be burned," teased Ba, looking wickedly at his sister, who cringed and wailed.

Just then, a man came down the pine tree hill. He was about to pass the bamboo clump, when, suddenly, he stopped. The man circled the bamboo trees, his hand resting on a big knife tucked in his belt.

He looked at Mama Bamboo's waist. "Too thick," he muttered to himself.

"Watch out," Mama Bamboo whispered. "He's out to cut one of us."

Boo, Ba, and Bamba stood motionless.

The man bent Boo's six legs and Ba's ten arms. "Too hard," he said, shaking his head.

He bent Bamba backward until her head reached the ground, and then let her snap back all the way. "Just right," he declared, and started to chop her off her roots.

"Oh ooo oh," Bamba cried, not from the pain of her cuts but because she realized she would be taken away from her mother. She scratched the man's face with her stiff fingers.

"No, no, don't take our baby sister," Boo and Ba pleaded, but the man couldn't hear them.

"My poor child," Mama Bamboo sobbed. But she had always known that one day, she or her children would be cut down, and so she said consolingly, "You'll get your wish, Bamba. He'll make you into a Christmas tree. Don't cry. One day we'll find you."

The man was now dragging her up the hill.
Boo and Ba called after her, "Goodbye, Bamba! We
love you!"

The man piled Bamba on top of the pine trees at
the back of his truck. Bamba wriggled and wriggled
until she rolled herself towards the edge of the truck
and fell to the ground. Calmly, the man put her back.
She pushed herself off again. So he moved her to the
front seat beside him and drove off.

The man sang softly as the truck rumbled down
the hill. The forest scent of the pine trees soothed
Bamba. Soon she was asleep.

Hours later, she opened her eyes. The truck had
stopped! The man unloaded the pine trees and
fastened each to a stout wooden post, so that they
stood perfectly straight and tall.

Then he carried Bamba out of his truck. He
looked at her from every angle, and she preened,
fluttering her leaves. Suddenly, he lopped off her
outer leaves and twigs. He continued to prune her
until only Bamba's body and main arms remained.

Bamba grew afraid that he would turn her into a
pile of barbecue sticks for he started splitting her into
slim stalks.

She stuck a sliver into his finger. He quietly
fished it out.

Finally, he stopped cutting and started bending her this way and that, lashing her ends together here and there. Then he glued pieces of white, gold, and silver tinsel all over her, and she thought, *Oh, yes, I'm going to be a Christmas tree!*

But instead of planting her on a stand, he hung her at a window.

"Look at that! Isn't that beautiful?"

And Bamba saw, below the window, children jumping up and down on the grass, pointing at her.

The breeze gave her a little nudge, and in the glass window of the house across the narrow street, she saw herself. She looked like a star, a glorious star!

That night, a light within her glowed. And Bamba the Christmas lantern gazed across the town to where her mother and brothers were, and she knew that they could see her too.

Maya and Tamaraw

AYA and Tamaraw were great friends. Wherever Tamaraw went, you could be sure that Maya was not far behind.

Whenever Tamaraw bathed in the mountain spring, Maya would sit on his back and sing:

> *"He may be big and I am small,*
> *But that doesn't bother me.*
> *Not at all.*
> *We are friends…we are friends.*
> *I love Tamaraw and he loves me."*

Whenever Tamaraw foraged in the forest, Maya

would sit in a tree and sing:

> *"He may be big and I am small,*
> *But that doesn't bother me.*
> *Not at all.*
> *We are friends…we are friends,*
> *I love Tamaraw and he loves me."*

Tamaraw looked like his cousin, Carabao. But he was smaller and his graceful horns formed the letter "V" on his head. He lived in the wilds of Mindoro, never having ventured beyond its borders.

Maya was a little brown bird that once lived in the town of Calapan near the forests of Mindoro. The noise and the smoke of the town had driven her into the forest where she met Tamaraw.

One day Tamaraw came home with a frown set right between his brown horns and said, "I saw stars where the mountain flattens and the sky meets the plains."

"Stars on the ground?" asked the puzzled little bird.

"Yes. But they're not as shiny or beautiful as those we see in the sky," answered Tamaraw. "Do you suppose they're fallen stars?"

Maya saw that her friend was troubled.

Tamaraw knew just about everything there was

to know about the forest. It was Tamaraw who had taught Maya just where to find the sweetest water. He knew where the juiciest worms were hidden. He knew which plants could be turned into umbrellas when it rained.

"Maybe you can show me the stars," said Maya.

So Tamaraw set off with Maya on his back to the place with the fallen stars. On the way, Maya sang:

> *"He may be big and I am small,*
> *But that doesn't bother me.*
> *Not at all.*
> *We are friends…we are friends,*
> *I love Tamaraw and he loves me."*

Finally they reached the place that had confused Tamaraw.

"Oh, Tamaraw!" Maya said. "Those are not stars but the lights from the town of Calapan where I used to live."

"Do they twinkle like the stars in the sky? And do they hide when it rains?" asked Tamaraw.

"No," answered Maya. "Those lights come on only at night to help people see what they are doing. Come, let's get a little closer so you can see the town."

Maya and Tamaraw went closer for a better view.

The little town of Calapan was celebrating the Christmas season and it was bustling with activity. Maya, who had seen all this before, explained what was happening.

"Soon the church bell will ring and all the people will come out to hear *misa de gallo*." said Maya.

"Clang…clang…clang!" the church bell called.

Tamaraw didn't like the sound, but he didn't say a word.

Maya continued, "Once the mass is over, the people will come out and celebrate. They will have *puto bumbong* and *bibingka* and wash all that down with *salabat*.

"They will do this everyday until Christmas." Maya said. Maya was proud she could teach Tamaraw something.

Tamaraw, who knew when the rains would come and the sun would set, remained silent and listened.

He was proud of his little friend. Maya was a smart bird.

"Let's go home, Maya," called Tamaraw. He had heard enough about the village.

For the first time Maya did not follow Tamaraw. She just stood there, watching.

"Tamaraw…" Maya began slowly. "I miss my

home in the church tower. I miss the voices of the children and the noises of the village."

Tamaraw listened quietly with a growing heaviness of heart.

"I miss the lights of the village at dusk before I close my eyes to rest," said Maya.

"But what of the stars in the sky?" answered Tamaraw. "Are they not more beautiful than these at their best?

"And what of the noises of the village? Are not the sounds of dripping mountain water and the wind whispering in the trees more restful than these?"

"Have we not found a place to live among all the creatures of the forest?" asked Tamaraw.

"Maya," said Tamaraw. "As you know, there are probably very few like myself left. But I have found a friend in you, as you have found in me. I will miss you if you go." Tamaraw awaited her reply with bated breath.

The little bird grew pensive. After a period of silence, she finally said, "Tamaraw, I may miss the church tower, the children, and the lights, but if I left I would miss you most of all. We are friends and friends belong together."

At hearing her words, the heavy feeling in his chest disappeared. Tamaraw smiled with relief.

And so Maya and Tamaraw returned home to the forest. As Tamaraw walked, Maya sat on his back and sang:

> *"He may be big and I am small,*
> *But that doesn't bother me.*
> *Not at all.*
> *We are friends…we are friends.*
> *I love Tamaraw and he loves me."*

KITO AND THE BAMBOO ORGAN

ITO looked at his reflection in the mirror and noticed the dark shadow on his upper lip. He was growing a mustache! Even his hands were no longer soft and smooth, but hard and callused like those of a young man.

Kito liked growing up. But he dreaded the time when he would have to leave the choir because his voice was changing. Father Manuel, the musical director, had begun auditioning the younger boys for the choir.

Kito was part of the Las Piñas Boys Choir that sang along with the Bamboo Pipe Organ in the huge old church in Las Piñas. Kito had been singing with the choir for nearly half his life. He was now thirteen.

Kito often had to miss a party or a favorite TV show to attend choir practice. But that didn't bother him, for the sound of the bamboo organ was always enough to make him happy.

Kito knew that the Las Piñas Bamboo Organ was the only one of its kind in the world and that it was very old. The organ was completed in 1823 by a Spanish missionary, Fray Diego Cerra. He also knew that the bamboo organ was made of more than one thousand bamboo pipes that had been buried in the sand for many years. This hardened the pipes, making them immune to termites.

Everyday Kito would come to church to polish the smooth, yellowish keys. He often touched the organ's grayish-green pipes. To him, the bamboo was a magical plant that held the secret to beautiful music.

Whenever the organ played, it became a living, breathing thing, producing the purest, sweetest sounds Kito had ever heard.

Tap! Tap! Tap! went the baton. Father Manuel raised his hands for silence, then gave the signal to sing. The choir was practicing for the Christmas Eve Mass that would end the nine-day *misa de gallo*.

How Kito enjoyed these dawn masses! Singing

in the choir loft made him feel very important.

As soon as the church bells began ringing at three in the morning, Kito would be up and about. It was he who prepared the *salabat* his family looked for as soon as they got out of bed.

It would already be time to leave just as his mother was coming out from under the mosquito net, still sleepy-eyed and groggy.

"Son, you will sing well today, I know," she would always say. But Mama knew that her son was no longer a child.

As he walked under the branches of an enormous tree, now glowing with *capiz* lanterns, Kito felt a heaviness in his heart. Not only was it Christmas Eve, it was also the time when Father Manuel announced who would remain in the choir.

He took his place beside his choirmates.

Mariano nudged him. "Looks like it'll be our last day today." Mariano was Kito's age, and he too knew that he would have to be replaced. Already Mariano was spending more time in the town plaza trying out for the basketball team.

Soon the choirboys filled the church with their voices, and the bamboo organ sang along with them.

For as long as he could remember, the bamboo organ was always a great part of his town's Christmas festivities. Christmas without the bamboo organ was like a forest without trees.

The mass ended sooner than he would have liked. Kito felt the bamboo organ had outdone itself that night and had played the last solo especially for him.

Now it was time for Father Manuel's announcement. "Kito Mejia," Father Manuel called out. Kito knew this was it. His hands grew clammy and his breath quickened.

"Kito, I will let you stay on," Father Manuel began. Kito could hardly believe what the good priest was saying. What did he want with an unsteady, deepening voice? Most of the songs were suited to younger voices. Father Manuel was very strict and selective with the boys in the choir.

"I have watched you grow and I know you love working with the bamboo organ, Kito," the priest continued. "So I have decided that you are to stay with us, but no longer as a choirboy. You will stay on to learn more about the bamboo organ." Father Manuel's eyes were twinkling now.

"When you are old enough, we will send you abroad to learn all about pipe organs. The bamboo organ is quite old and delicate. I will need someone special to take very good care of it."

Father Manuel took Kito's hand. "Merry Christmas, Kito!"

"Thank you, Father, and Merry Christmas!"

Kito couldn't have hoped for a better gift. It was a merry Christmas, indeed!

BITUIN THE PAROL

 IT's coming! It's coming! Christmas is coming!

The Christmas shop in the huge shopping mall in Manila was ready to open. Everyone was terribly excited.

"I'll be bought first!" announced Pine Tree confidently. He stood at the very center of the shop.

"I came from a dark forest, where even the sunbeams couldn't touch the ground because my branches blocked them!" boasted Pine Tree. "Then I flew in an airplane. It was such a long trip and it took me far away from my home." *SWISHHH!* Pine Tree's huge branches spread out like a plane's wings.

"Nobody can shine like we do!" chorused the Fairy Lights, twinkling around the room. First they were blue, then red, then yellow, then pink, then green, then violet.

"Well I have chocolate icing! Mmm, yummy!" bragged miniature Chocolate House.

"We were made by the best artists in the world," piped in the delicate figurines in the *belen*.

And so everyone in the Christmas shop talked about how shiny or how big or how bright they were.

All except a *capiz parol*. Her name was Bituin.

Bituin thought herself neither as fine or flashy as the others, so she kept to herself.

Until Pine Tree noticed.

"Hey, little star, what's your story?" he asked.

And so, Bituin talked about herself.

"My home lies in shallow waters, where the river meets the sea. I lived there with my family among other oyster families.

"One day a little boy and his father came to our riverbed to collect the whitest and brightest shells. You see, the inner layer of an oyster shell is made of a hard pearly iridescent substance called *capiz*. When the boy and his father had gathered enough capiz shells they glued these together to form a star—that's me!"

"What happened then, Bituin?" asked Candy Cane, surprised to find that Bituin was made of shells.

"After that, I was borne on a pole and paraded along with other lanterns in the Lantern Festival," Bituin said proudly.

"Hrrmmph...show-off!" said Fairy Lights, turning a deep green.

Bituin ignored Fairy Lights. "The Lantern Festival in Pampanga takes place every Christmas," explained Bituin. "Everyone in the barrios works together to make a lantern. A barrio without a lantern is considered a disgrace," she continued.

"The biggest lanterns are paraded all over town in cars or jeepneys. Later, the best are awarded prizes." Bituin began to glow now that everyone was listening. "It was now time for the big bonfire!"

"Bonfire?" asked Pine Tree, shuddering.

"The winners were burned so that they couldn't be duplicated for the following festival."

"Why didn't they burn you too?" asked golden Christmas Ball hanging in the window.

"Oh, no! I was wrapped in a big box and here I am!" Bituin beamed happily.

Just then a little boy and his mother walked into the shop.

"Mommy, I want that one!" the little boy said, pointing right at Bituin. "It's beautiful and it'll look just right outside my window. Now everyone will know they are welcome in our home."

As soon as they arrived home the little boy promptly hung Bituin outside his bedroom window.

On Christmas Eve, a family of three, exhausted from a long journey, paused in their tracks by the little boy's home, their faces illuminated by the warm, inviting light that shone from the capiz parol.

THE AETA
CHRISTMAS BABY

 E had doe eyes—soft, sad, deep-brown eyes. He was staring hungrily at the pot of rice Cocoy, Luding, and Tan-Tan were sharing.

Luding beckoned to the child. He ate desperately without saying a word. Not even the mothers could guess how old he was. He was as tiny as four-year-old Tan-Tan, but as quick as ten-year-old Cocoy. Cocoy started affectionately calling the child "Maeta," short for *matá* and *Aeta*. It became his name.

None of the refugees in the *lahar* wasteland of Zambales knew how the Aeta child came to join them. Suddenly he was in their cramped tent.

Mang Ambo, the village sage, said: "The volcano

god Pinatubo spewed his anger all over our homes and our fields, but our families are alive and together. But this poor child has lost everyone and everything he ever had."

It was Christmas Eve. The volcano was resting quietly and the wind had stopped blowing fine white ash over the tents. The smell of sulfur had weakened. Some relief workers had promised to arrive with a truck to transport the refugees to a place where they could begin life anew, but they had not come in what seemed an eternity.

"I never thought I'd miss my godchildren coming by on Christmas day to kiss my hand, *'Mano po, Ninong!'* I'd empty my pockets for them," Mang Ambo said. "I'd be such a poor man after Christmas," he chuckled. "*'Sus*, I miss even that!"

Everyone gathered around the circle of light cast by the solitary kerosene lamp. The children nestled against their parents; Maeta snuggled against Cocoy.

Cocoy's mother said, "I miss the *panunuluyan*."

"What's that?" the children asked.

"It's the Christmas Eve street play. The town is the stage. Townsfolk are chosen to play Joseph and Mary, Herod, the Magi, shepherds, angels, choristers, and innkeepers."

"What do they do?" inquired Tan-Tan.

"Joseph and Mary walk to each of the houses chosen to represent inns and ask for shelter. The innkeepers turn Mary and Joseph away with many excuses," Cocoy's mother explained.

"And then?" Cocoy prompted.

"At last, Mary says she cannot go any further. Angels console her. Someone offers them a stable which is actually the *belen* in the darkened church. The baby is born at midnight. A star descends from the choir loft to the roof of the stable. The whole church suddenly lights up! Angels sing Gloria! The boys in the belfry ring all the bells. And the midnight mass begins."

All were quiet with thoughts of past Christmases.

Then Cocoy, who couldn't keep still for very long, jumped up. "Let's do the panunuluyan!" he said, excited by the idea of a new game. "Luding! You'll be Mary. I'll be Joseph."

"What about me?" Tan-Tan didn't want to be left out.

"You can be a shepherd," Cocoy said.

Suddenly everyone wanted to take part. "Pretend that my poor corner here is the biggest inn ever," Mang Ambo said. "I'll be the first innkeeper."

"I'll be the second," offered an old man.

"We'll be the Three Kings!" Three young men jostled one another, laughing.

"The Baby Jesus," Cocoy reminded them, "Who'll be Baby Jesus?"

And everyone agreed, "The child! Maeta! He'll be our Baby!"

Maeta smiled as he saw everyone smiling at him.

And so it was a merry group the relief workers found, not the despairing people they had expected to pick up that Christmas Eve.

THE CHRISTMAS GHOSTS OF VIGAN

REE—EEE—EAK!

Noella turned around. She was sure she had heard the narra floor creak.

But no one was there. She looked up. Maring, the cook's nine-year-old daughter, was watching her closely. Maring leaned over the *sungca* game between them and whispered, "Careful. There are ghosts here."

Noella felt the skin on her arms tingle.

"Don't worry. They won't harm you," Maring assured her with a twinkle in her eye. "They're happy ghosts."

"*Happy* ghosts?" Noella asked with more than a hint of disbelief.

"They're all over Vigan. This was a rich, carefree place during the Spanish colonial period. The people who lived here a long time ago come back whenever there's a fiesta. And they have fun all over again! Like now, Christmas time."

Oh no, Noella thought. *Why did I agree when Papa and Mama suggested that I come ahead to Lola's house? I hope Papa finishes his work so they can come soon.*

At dinner that evening, Noella and her lola sat at the long molave table in the main dining room.

Noella turned her heavy silver spoon over and over. How many people, now dead, had used this very spoon before her?

Lola peered at Noella through her thick eyeglasses.

"Is something wrong?" she asked.

"Lola, Maring says there are ghosts here."

"In all my seventy years, I've never seen a ghost," chuckled Lola.

"The floor creaked, as if someone we couldn't see were walking on it," blurted Noella.

"*Ay apo*! Wood expands and contracts as it warms and cools during the day and night. That's what makes a house creak."

Noella slept in Lola's room that night. At three in the morning, Lola woke Noella. "It's time for *misa de gallo*, Noella. Up, up, we mustn't be late!"

The night was chilly and hung heavily on the narrow, cobblestoned streets. Lola, Noella, Itas, the cook, and Maring walked past old stone houses with *capiz* and iron-grilled windows. People flocked to the cathedral, all alight for the celebration.

The fragrance of *pianono* and *londres* pastries and *chocolate eh* steaming in nipa stalls around the plaza greeted them as they stepped out of church after mass. People were milling about. *Surely*, thought Noella, *there couldn't be any ghosts here!*

She was feverish the day before Christmas. Lola put her to bed in the breezy tower bedroom where she had a view of the whole town. Noella dozed, awoke, sipped some water, and napped again.

When she roused herself from sleep, Maring was sitting on the bed beside her. "Look!" Maring pointed out the window.

Noella walked to the window. She saw the town of Vigan bustling underneath. Was something amiss?

"Come!" Maring offered Noella her hand. She took it, and both girls floated out the window effortlessly, as if someone had given each of them a pair of wings.

For several minutes, they hovered over the town, eventually alighting on the branch of a *salamagui* tree.

Then it dawned on Noella that there weren't any cars, only horses and *calesas*. Men wore loose, collarless shirts and wide pants. Women wore *kimonas*, wide skirts, and beaded slippers that click-clacked as they walked. People cooked in groups under the trees, stirring cauldrons over open fires, and roasting pigs on spits.

They listened to a man strumming a *banduria* and singing his comic version of *Pamulinawen*, which he teasingly dedicated to a white-haired lady named Soledad. How the cooks laughed! Soledad looked up and saw Noella and Maring on the topmost branch of the salamagui tree. "Come down!" she invited. "Come taste the *tupig*!"

The tupig were molasses-coconut rice cakes, bundled in layers of banana leaves, and roasted in a pile of burning rice chaff. The kind old lady gave the girls one each.

"Don't eat it now," Maring whispered, "or we'll never escape from this ghost-world."

"What do you mean?" Noella started to ask, but just as she tucked the tupig in her pocket, she was back in bed, and Papa and Mama were hugging her awake. Maring sat quietly on the window sill.

Noella's fever was gone. She looked out the window. The town was noisier. Cars and jeepneys careened dangerously down the roads. T-shirted men and short-skirted women, children in tow, went about on Christmas errands. Everything seemed as it had been before.

"What's wrong, child?" Papa asked.

"Nothing," Noella murmured. "I just had a dream."

She felt in her pocket with apprehension. The tupig was there! She offered it to her parents before she took a bite herself. "Mmmm! Yummy," Mama said. "This is so good! Where did you get it?"

Maring and Noella exchanged glances. Maring reached into her pocket and took out her tupig. And they both smiled.

THE POOR MAN WHO BECAME KING

DA had lost her mother at a very tender age and was brought up by her father. She simply adored him. She thought he was the most handsome, strong, and caring father of all.

One cool evening in December, father and daughter sat at the bamboo table in their nipa hut by the sea.

"Guess what I heard in school? It's time again to choose people to play the Three Kings for our town fiesta. *Itay*, why don't they ever pick you?" Ida pondered out loud.

Her father laughed. "I am a poor fisherman. Only the rich or important people are chosen."

"But the sea is often dangerous, and fishing is important, and you do it better than anyone here in our barrio...or the little islands of Gaspar, Melchor, and Baltazar...or all of Marinduque for that matter!" the little girl insisted.

"So long as I am a king to you," her father said, chuckling, "that's enough for me!"

Ida spooned the *maya-maya* fish soup she had prepared into her father's bowl. A gingery smell rose from the clay pot. "Itay, I have this feeling that something wonderful will happen on the Feast of the Three Kings.

"Doesn't something wonderful happen every year? Our sleepy town wakes up! More tourists come. There's a play in the plaza about the Three Kings. It has Herod in his palace, and the Christ Child in the stable gets better and better every year! And the parade! The Three Kings on their white horses, the children marching to the band music, and people throwing coins and candies from their windows!"

"But child," said her father. "I will not allow you to follow the Three Kings all around town like you did last year. You came home well past midnight, remember?"

"If you were to be King, you wouldn't have to

worry because I would be with you all the time," Ida said. "I wonder why I have this feeling that something special, really special will happen."

Early the next morning, Ida sat on the cool sand at the beach. She was on the lookout for her father's boat. When her father landed with his catch, she would sort the fish and help him carry the heavy baskets to market.

A child had been playing on a raft in the shallow water. Suddenly, Ida realized that the raft had floated out into open sea, into a place where she knew there to be a powerful undertow. She looked around. There was no one else.

She ran into the water and furiously swam for the raft. Her father had taught her to swim with all her strength. *Hurry, hurry! Faster, faster!* she told herself.

The child started to scream. Ida was near enough to see the fear on his face.

She grabbed for the raft. It tilted as the child scrambled toward her. He slid into the water. She reached for his arm but missed as he thrashed about. Taking hold of his shirt, she lifted his head above water. She said, as calmly as she could, "I'm here. Now hold on to the raft, not my neck."

The undertow is close by, she thought. *God help me!*

But now she was in control. Swimming with one arm, the other arm steered the raft ahead of her. She made it to shore!

The child's mother ran to them, crying, "Miguel, Miguel!" She clasped him to her bosom. "I told you never to go into the water all by yourself. You could have drowned!"

That evening the mayor came to their home just as Ida and her father were about to have dinner. "Your daughter saved my son," he said. "I cannot thank her enough, but I must try." He turned to the little girl. "Ida, what can I do for you?"

Ida could not answer.

"Please," the mayor implored. "Tell me."

"My father gives me everything I need," she said shyly. "But if you will let him ride as one of the Three Kings...."

And that is how a poor fisherman became King for a night and a day. With a red velvet robe on his broad shoulders and a gold crown on his head, he looked as though he had been born to be King Gaspar. Ida walked proudly beside him, clothed in flowing white, with flowers in her hair and angel's wings strapped lightly on her back.

The Sultan with a Heart of Stone

MAR and his father, Abdul Qadir, arrived at the Maranao village before dawn. In the dimness, Omar saw houses on stilts at the edge of the lake where the great sails of the *vintas* rested. Inland, the pointed dome of the mosque soared to meet the half-lit sky. The *bilal*, the man in the minaret, was calling everyone to *azan*, to pray and give praise to Allah.

As the sun rose, Omar momentarily forgot the fear he had tried to hide from his father. He had not wanted to come, but his father had asked him to, and he loved his father very dearly.

A happy glow brightened the village. This was the great festival of the *Eid'l Fitr*, the end of the long fast of the holy month of Ramadan. This was a joyous time of the year for gift-giving, and sharing with the poor; a time for visiting loved ones; and a time when enemies forgave each other.

"Eid'l Fitr!" people greeted Omar.

The women wore new *malong*s, woven in patterns of the deepest greens, tangerines, fuschias, scarlets, and golds. The men were in loose white shirts and pants. Even the houses were newly painted, their outer beams carved in glorious scrolls, like the magnificent prows of boats.

So this is where the story began, thought Omar, the story his father and mother had told him over and over throughout the years, beginning with his fifth birthday. He never tired of hearing it, for delightful bits were added with the retelling, and the ending changed now and then.

Once upon a time there lived a Muslim prince, the eldest son of the Sultan. Everyone agreed that he was all that a prince should be. He was kind and strong, and he was determined to learn all that a Muslim prince should know because, someday, he would be Sultan, charged with the care of his people.

He rode a horse as if he and the horse were one with the wind. He sailed a vinta as if he and the boat were one with the sea. He learned the Koran as well as anyone who was not an imam, or high priest, could.

His entire life had been planned for him. And a crucial part of that plan was that he was to marry a Muslim princess. That was where he went astray, or so people said.

Like many of the young Muslim men, he was sent to study in Manila, far away from his Maranao home. There he met an enchanting Christian woman. He fell in love with her, and she with him.

"And so they were married...." Omar's father and mother said, seemingly ending the story.

"And lived happily ever after?" Omar asked, for his question was part of the ritual of the storytelling.

"Yes, happily every after." His father laughed and added: "And they had a son named Omar."

"Was the prince's name Abdul Qadir?" Omar asked. "And his wife's name Anna?" His parents nodded yes. Omar was delighted with the story of his own life.

Two years later his parents added to the story: "By marrying the Christian woman, the Muslim prince had made his father, the Sultan, very angry. One day the prince would return to the village of his birth and ask for his father's forgiveness."

Another two years passed. Omar's parents still
had more to add. "The prince's son, who had grown
to be a fine boy, would be his father's messenger.
Alone, he would go to his grandfather, the Sultan,
with his father's plea for forgiveness. For it was
known, far and wide, that the Sultan had the softest
heart for children."

Inside the mosque, the prayers for the Eid'l Fitr
were over.

"It is time, Omar." his father said.

"Why can't you come with me?" Omar asked,
though he knew the answer.

"I hurt my father very deeply, Omar," his father
answered. "By marrying against his wishes, he felt as
though I had betrayed him. He has closed his heart
to me. My father is a stubborn man, Omar. He will
not listen to me, much less look at me. To him, I do
not exist. But how can your grandfather still think
my marriage a mistake when faced with such a fine
grandson?"

Omar looked up at his father, and their dark eyes
locked for a moment in understanding.

The Sultan sat imposingly on his throne at the end of
a long, grand hall. Omar walked slowly, his head held

proud under the *kopya* or fez, his shoulders broad under the long-sleeved white shirt, "a Maranao prince's shirt," his father had said.

It was quiet and solemn. The scent of spices came from somewhere within.

Omar was face-to-face with the Sultan. He felt fear well up inside him. For a fleeting instant, Omar wanted to turn around and run away. But he saw the Sultan's eyes. They were just like his father's. He took courage.

"I kiss your hand, Grandfather," Omar said.

"Who are you?" the Sultan rumbled.

"I am the son of your son, Abdul Qadir," Omar replied.

"I have no son by that name."

"My father begs to remind you that it is the feast of forgiveness."

"What do you know of the Eid'l Fitr? You know nothing of Islam."

"My father taught me that Islam means obeying the will of Allah; that there are Five Articles of Faith: belief in one god, belief in angels, belief in the Revealed Books, belief in Mohammed and his fore-runners, and belief in the Day of Judgement. There are Five Pillars…" Omar paused to take a deep breath, "of Islam…."

With a wave of his hand, the Sultan stopped Omar. "Come closer," the Sultan commanded, "that I may look at you."

The Sultan looked at Omar from head to foot.

"You have your father's eyes and bearing," the Sultan murmured at last. "Tell my son, Abdul Qadir, to come to me."

Omar's heart leapt with joy at hearing his grandfather's words. And the young boy dreamed of the day he would bring his mother to meet the Sultan. And from that day on, they would all live happily together as a family.

BINNY AND THE
COCONUT MAN

ON'T!" Binny looked up from the Christmas wreath he was making from silvery *sinamay* and pointed to the coconut tree outside. The tree had an unusually fat trunk. Coconuts and round green *capiz* lanterns hung from its branches. "Please don't cut the tree! It's his home! And Christmas is almost here!" Binny pleaded.

Papa frowned and stuck a fork into a slippery slice of papaya. "Not again, Binny. There are no such creatures as little men living in tree trunks. The tree has to give way for the swimming pool," Papa said.

"You're late for school," Mama gently reminded.

That afternoon Binny came home to find Mama

and the gardener standing by the coconut tree. The capiz lanterns lay on the grass. The gardener picked up a heavy axe.

"Stop, stop!" Binny rushed to hug the tree. The gardener looked at Binny's mother questioningly.

Binny reached into a hollow in the trunk. A damp smell came from within. "I told you, Mama, this is his front door!"

Mama sighed. "My son thinks a little man lives in this tree."

The gardener dropped his axe. "Bad luck to cut down a *duwende*'s tree, and good luck to let it be," he said. "That's what my grandfather used to say." With that he picked up the lanterns and hung them up again on the branches.

The moon smiled on the tree at dinnertime, and the lanterns glimmered like lighted coconuts.

"Have they cut down that tree yet?" Papa asked, scowling. "The men are coming tomorrow to dig the swimming pool."

Mama looked at Binny out of the corner of her eye. "I'll explain later," she replied.

At bedtime Binny sat on his bed and switched his lamp on and off, then on again. He waited for an answer to his signal.

The window creaked open. The Coconut Man

jumped in. *Thuk, thuk.* His head resembled a husked coconut, with three coin-sized nodes that were close-set eyes and an "O"-shaped mouth. He didn't seem to have a nose.

The smell of moist earth followed him.

"Hello, Binny," he said in a breathy voice. "I'm grateful to you for saving my home from the gardener's axe."

"Papa's cutting your tree tomorrow," Binny reported sadly. "Will you be able to find a new home before Christmas? And will you still come and play with me?"

"I cannot leave. There are no other suitable coconut trees in these parts. Many years ago, there were plenty of coconut trees. Everybody needed them—for coconut meat, coco milk, bowls, house posts, buckles, buttons. People even used coconut trees to hang hammocks from. Not anymore."

"Can't you just show yourself to Papa?" Binny wondered. "Ask him not to cut your tree down."

"No," answered the Coconut Man, "only certain boys and girls can see coconut people."

Suddenly the Coconut Man's face brightened. "What is your father's lucky number?"

"Seven," Binny replied. "Why?"

"I have a plan. Come with me!"

The wet grass squished beneath Binny's bare feet. Into the hollow of the coconut tree they went, up a narrow spiral staircase. At the top, the leaves brushed their faces and the coconuts and lanterns hung at their feet. The full moon laid a bluish veil over the house and the garden. Binny was breathless.

"Let's get to work," the Coconut Man said. He twisted a coconut around and off the tree. His knobby hands were surprisingly strong. He tossed it down the stairs. *Bog, bog, bog, bog.*

He gathered thirteen more coconuts. Binny hurled them like bowling balls down the stairs. Finally, their work was done. The Coconut Man gave Binny a drink of coconut water. It looked like melted moonlight in the halved coco shell.

Together they climbed down the tree. Binny bade the Coconut Man goodbye at his front door and stole back into his bedroom.

Binny awoke early the next morning. Papa and Mama were outside. On the steps, lined up neatly, were seven green and seven brown coconuts, each with a coconut leaf ribbon.

Papa looked bewildered. "How did they get here? A lucky double-seven...I don't believe it!" He gave his son a strange look. Then he announced with a smile, "All right, Binny, we're not cutting down the tree."

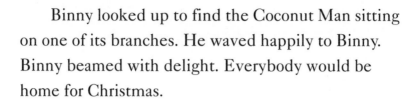

Binny looked up to find the Coconut Man sitting on one of its branches. He waved happily to Binny. Binny beamed with delight. Everybody would be home for Christmas.

THE
CHRISTMAS BELL

ONGG! BONNGG! BONNGGG!

The great church bell called to the sleeping town of Santa Maria, Ilocos Sur.

WAKE UP! WAKE UP! IT'S TIME...BONNGGG! the bell announced.

The sound traveled down the belfry, through the *kumbento* across the church, along the hillside, past the rice fields, and into the town.

BONGG! BONNGG! BONNGGG! It woke up the chickens, roused the pigs, and prodded the cows. It summoned fathers, mothers, children, and babies who cried in their cradles.

BONNGGG, BONNGGG, BONNGGG. WAKE UP! WAKE UP! IT'S TIME... The bell's call resounded across the Cordillera mountains and echoed down towards the ocean far below.

BONNGGG, BONNGGG. WAKE UP! WAKE UP! IT'S TIME…

Nuestra Señora de la Asuncion is one of the most beautiful old churches in the Philippines. Built in the seventeenth century, it stands atop a solitary hill overlooking the town. Visitors have to climb 86 steps to reach it. Constructed of grey stone and brick, the grand church is connected to a two-story kumbento by a stone bridge. The tower that holds the great bell stands several feet away.

During the Christmas season, the Spanish bell of Santa Maria rings each day at three o'clock in the morning, calling people to *misa de gallo*.

But there was one Christmas when the bell might not have rung, were it not for a young boy named Pepito.

Father Rafael had been parish priest of Nuestra Señora de la Asuncion for many years. He was always glad to see people attending mass so early in the morning. He even organized a marching band to go though town after the bell had rung, to help keep eveyone awake! Father Rafael cared a great deal for the townpeople and everybody loved him.

Every Christmas Father Rafael honored a boy from the village with the privilege of ringing the bell. This year he chose Pepito.

Ten-year-old Pepito was a handsome little boy with a curly mop of dark hair. He had large round eyes that took in everything around him.

Pepito slept on a mat in the kumbento hallway for the nine days of the misa de gallo. At first, it took quite some time to fall asleep. When the last candle was blown out, Pepito imagined that the statues of the saints lining the hallway were shrouded monsters in the dark. Frightened, Pepito hid under a warm *Iloko* blanket until sleep overtook him.

He would not have stayed, had it not been for the fried rice, *salabat*, and freshly-baked bread set aside for him every morning.

"Mama, I don't want to ring the bell anymore," Pepito complained.

"Patience, child," Mama would console him. "Don't you know it's an honor for one so young to ring the church bell for the misa de gallo? Very few young boys are given the chance."

That was true. Pepito was a superstar whenever he entered his classroom. His classmates all gawked at him, wondering what it felt like to ring the great bell.

"*Psssst*, Pepito," whispered Luis who sat beside him. "Were there ghosts last night?" Luis knew the stone steps on the other side of the church led to an old Spanish cemetery.

Pepito shrugged the question aside. He had been asking that himself.

On Christmas Eve, the last day of the dawn masses, Pepito was already up and about by the time Father Rafael came to rouse him.

"Pepito! You're awake!" Father Rafael smiled. "*Diyos ti agngina*," he said, ruffling the boys hair. "We've had a wonderful season this year!"

Pepito beamed. He knew just what the priest meant. Since he began ringing the bell, the church was always filled with people.

There was *Nanang* Tilyang all bundled up, her gnarled fingers moving endlessly as she prayed the rosary. There was *Tatang* Miguel stomping out his tobacco by the church door. And, of course, there were the infant twins, Herminia and Melinda, gurgling in their mother's arms as she held her handkerchief to a *santo niño*.

Pepito started to climb the long, narrow steps to the belfry. He had to go slowly as the stone steps were smooth and damp with dew, with cracks and breaks here and there. As he climbed, Pepito looked towards the sea, still as a pond, glinting in the moonlight.

Finally he reached the top. There it was—the great bell that had rung for many centuries. Once upon a time, Spanish kings sent bells to new towns created in the Philippines during their reign.

Pepito touched the cold, rough metal and traced the outline of the cross etched on its surface. It was put there because people believed the sound of the bell drove the devil away. For this reason, people liked to live, as they say, *bajo a la campaña.*

Pepito grasped the bell's rope and tugged, bracing himself for its metallic clang.

But the bell hung motionless.

Pepito tugged again. The bell refused to budge.

"Are you going to let me down *now?*" Pepito nearly screamed with panic. Never had there been a mass without its joyful ringing.

"Today is Christmas Eve!" Pepito yelled, frustrated. His heart thundered in his chest. He pulled on the heavy rope with all his might.

Still the bell did not move.

Father Rafael's marching band was now making as much noise as it could.

"Ring for me, please!" Pepito begged as he tugged and tugged.

It was five to three! Only five minutes remained. Four minutes...three...two...one...

Pepito prayed with all his heart.

And then summoning all his strength, he gave one last tug.

BONGG! BONNGG! BONNGGG! WAKE UP! WAKE UP! IT 'S TIME...BONGGG! Just in time for Christmas Eve Mass!

BONGG! BONNGG! BONNGGG! IT 'S TIME! The sound traveled down the belfry, through the kumbento across the church, along the hillside, past the rice fields, and into the town.

BONNGGG! BONNGGG! BONNGGG!

"*Cocka-doodle dooo!*" answered the roosters.

"*Wheeeeeee,*" neighed the horses.

"*Quack, quack, quack!*" cried the ducks.

Fathers washed up. Mothers rushed to the kitchen. Children jumped out of their beds. Babies cried in their cradles.

BONNGGG! BONNGGG! BONNGGG! The bell's call echoed throughout the Cordillera range and into the ocean below.

And that is how a boy named Pepito once saved Christmas in Santa Maria.

GLOSSARY

Aeta   an indigenous people of Central Luzon
Ay apo   "Oh Lord"

bajo a la campana   within the sound of the bells
banduria   mandolin
belen   crèche
bibingka   a rice-flour cake topped with carabao
    cheese and grated coconut
Bituin   Star

calesa   carriage
capiz   transluscent sea shell used for window
    panes and lamp shades
chocolate eh   thick Spanish hot chocolate

Diyos ti agngina   "The Lord will reward you"
duwende   dwarf

gulaman   gelatin

halo-halo   a dessert of sweetened beans, young rice,
    sugar palm seeds, bananas, jackfruit, gelatin,
    custard, and ice cream with crushed ice

Iloko   Ilocano
Itay   Father

kaong   sweetened sugar-palm seeds
kimona   a loose, native blouse worn by women
kumbento   priests' quarters

jeepney   an elongated passenger jeep

lahar   volcanic mud flow
leche flan   a dessert custard topped with caramel
lola   grandmother
londres   a small, sweet cake with a glazed top

malong   a sleeveless, draped garment used in
   Mindanao
Mang   a term of respect for an older man
Mano po, Ninong   "I pay my respects, Godfather"
matá   eyes
maya-maya   red snapper
misa de gallo   dawn mass
molave   a Philippine hardwood

Nanang   a term of respect for an older woman
nangka   jackfruit
narra   a Philippine hardwood
ninang   godmother
ninong   godfather
nipa hut   a thatched cottage
Nuestra Señora de la Asuncion   Our Lady of the
   Assumption

Pamulinawen   Ilocano folksong
panunuluyan   a Christmas play

parol Christmas lantern

Pasko ng mga Bata Children's Christmas

Pasko ng mga Binata't Dalaga Young People's
  Christmas

Pasko ng mga Matatanda The Elderly's Christmas

pianono a small, sandwich-shaped cake with a
  sweet filling

pinipig young rice

puto bumbong a purple-colored rice cake

sabá sweetened bananas

salabat ginger tea

salamagui tamarind

santo niño image of a child saint

sinamay a loosely woven cloth

sungca a traditional Filipino counting game played
  with cowrie shells

'Sus short for Jesus

Tatang a term of respect for elder men

tupig a coconut rice cake

vinta a small, swift boat with colorful sails, found
  in Mindanao

ABOUT THE AUTHORS

Lin Acacio-Flores received a bachelor's degree in music from the Holy Ghost College (now the College of the Holy Spirit). She completed a correspondence course at the Institute of Children's Literature in Connecticut, U.S.A. Ms. Flores was awarded two Don Carlos Palanca Memorial Awards for children's fiction and a Honolulu Magazine-Parker Pen Award for adult fiction. A free-lancer, her stories and articles have appeared in various magazines, including the *Sunday Inquirer Magazine*. She writes a column for *Parents* magazine. She is a member of Kuting, an organization devoted to children's literature.

Annette Flores Garcia graduated from the University of the Philippines with a bachelor's degree in journalism. A recent convert to creative writing, she also worked as a writer in corporate communications. Her children's stories and articles have appeared in the *Sunday Inquirer Magazine* and *Parents*. Ms. Garcia is a member of Kuting.

About the Artist

Albert Gamos is a seasoned artist with over a hundred publications to his name. A graduate of the University of the East School of Music and Arts, he ventured into film and advertising before he began to illustrate and design books for children.

Known for his rich and witty illustrations, he has won numerous awards. In 1992 he was recognized by the Philippine Board on Books for Young People for his outstanding contributions to children's book illustration and design.